CHOWDER

CHOWDER LOSES HIS HAT

STINKY LOVE

EGMONT

We bring stories to life

First published in Great Britain 2010
by Egmont UK Limited
239 Kensington High Street, London W8 6SA

Adapted by Brenda Apsley
Based on original storylines by C. H. Greenblatt,
Mike Bell and Tom King

ISBN 978 1 4052 5541 7

1 3 5 7 9 10 8 6 4 2

Printed and bound in Great Britain by the CPI Group

FSC

Mixed Sources
Product group from well-managed
forests and other controlled sources

Cert no. TT-COC-002332
www.fsc.org
© 1996 Forest Stewardship Council

Egmont is passionate about helping to preserve the world's remaining ancient forests.
We only use paper from legal and sustainable forest sources.

This book is made from paper certified by the Forestry Stewardship Council (FSC),
an organisation dedicated to promoting responsible management of forest resources.
For more information on the FSC, please visit www.fsc.org. To learn more about
Egmont's sustainable paper policy, please visit www.egmont.co.uk/ethical

CHOWDER LOSES HIS HAT

Chapter One

It was morning in Marzipan City, and Chowder was amusing himself by throwing his beloved purple hat – the one that looked like upside-down stuffed trouser legs, with added lumpy-bumpy bits – onto his pet stink cloud, Kimchi. And failing.

"Rats!" said Chowder as his hat flew off to the right. "OK, let's try again."

Faarp! went Kimchi, letting out one of his very rude, smelly noises.

Chowder tossed his hat again, but to the left. "Gotcha!" he said. And missed.

Fweep! went Kimchi.

"Rats!" Chowder repeated, throwing it again. Too far this time.

"Gonna getcha!" he said – but he didn't. Too close.

Fluurp! went Kimchi.

"Rats!" snarled Chowder.

He tried one more time. "Aha!" he said as the hat flew towards Kimchi, who was floating very still – but somehow it was too right, left, far and close all at the same time.

"Rats!" Chowder was really fed up now. "I thought playing 'Throw a Hat on Kimchi' would be easier than this." Then he had an idea. "Hey, I know, Kimchi. Maybe if you fly around really superfast, I'll have a better chance?"

Faarp! went Kimchi, obediently zipping around as Chowder tossed his hat. He missed again. But this time, his beloved hat sailed out the window!

"*My hat!*" screamed Chowder, running out on to the balcony. "Maybe it'll blow back?"

It did blow back – "*Yes!*" – but then blew away again before Chowder could grab it. "*Noooo!*"

This time, the hat didn't come back. Fearing the worst, Chowder and Kimchi rushed out to look for it. Chowder just wouldn't be the same cat/bear/rabbit without his hat. It was his very favourite hat. And, not to mention, his only one.

"OK, Kimchi," said Chowder gravely. "It's really important that we find my hat."

Faarp! went Kimchi.

"Really, really important."

Faarp-faarp! Kimchi repeated.

"Really, really, *really*, important." Chowder said again. Just to make sure Kimchi truly understood.

He did. **Faarpy-faarp-faarp!** If a stink cloud could sound a little miffed, Kimchi did.

But Chowder hadn't finished yet. "*Really, really, really, really, really, really, really, really ...*"

Faarp! went Kimchi. **Fweep! Fluurp!** He was getting angry now, and even more stinky.

"OK, OK," said Chowder. "Just so you know that it's really, really, really, really, really, really, really, really ..."

FAAAAAARP! farped Kimchi. He sounded as if he was about to explode. Messily. Smellily.

Chowder ignored him. "Now, if I were my hat, where would I be?" he said. "Aha!"

Chowder felt around on the top of his head. But ... no hat. "Drat, it's not up there," he said. "Hey, Kimchi, maybe you could track it down with your keen sense of smell? Luckily, I never wash my hat, so it should be easy for you to find."

Faarp! agreed Kimchi. Anything to shut him up. He sniffed a big sniff, then dashed off.

"Go get 'im, boy," encouraged Chowder. "Go get my hat!"

Kimchi quickly came back with something really smelly.

"Uh, I don't know, Kimchi," said Chowder. "That doesn't look much like my hat. I think it's just a smelly man."

Faarp! went Kimchi. *Oops*.

"'Just a smelly man?' *'Just a smelly man?'*" said the smelly man angrily, holding out a gold trophy. "You see this? I won first place in a garlic-eating competition. I am a smelly *champion*!"

Phee-ew! When he breathed in the smelly man's stinky breath, Chowder's face folded in on itself. No wonder the man won the contest!

When he had recovered, Chowder went on searching for his hat. He and Kimchi looked everywhere.

"Hat! Hat!" called Chowder. "Hey, Hat, where are you?"

Chowder grabbed a hat from a passerby to check whether it was his. But *oops* – there was a tiny man sitting in a bathtub under it.

The mini-bather made very angry mini-bather noises, so Chowder quickly put the hat back.

By now, he was getting sad and frustrated. "We're never going to find my hat," he said. "I guess I'll just have to live a hatless life. But what kind of a life is that?" Just thinking about it brought tears to his eyes. He flopped on the ground in despair. "Boo-hoo," he blubbed.

Faarp-faarp! Kimchi felt sorry for his owner, and floated up onto Chowder's head.

"Oh, thanks, Kimchi," sobbed Chowder. "It's sweet of you to wanna be my hat, but it's not the same ..."

Chowder gave a deep sigh. His beloved hat was good for so many things. It kept his head warm and smelly. It was the perfect size for a helping of Thrice Cream on a hot (or cold) day. And once, it had even taught him how to surf.

Would he ever see it again?

Chapter Two

As Chowder moped on the street, Kimchi noticed a hat walking by. A familiar hat. A purple hat. A hat with lumpy-bumps. *Chowder's hat!*

But it was someone else's hat now. A very small voice was singing from underneath it.

"Dingaloo, dingalee, what a day to be me!" sang the voice.

Faarp! went Kimchi, trying to attract Chowder's attention. **Fweep! Fluurp!**

Finally, Chowder looked up. His bulgy eyes bulged even more. "Hey, that's my hat!"

Suddenly, the hat ran away. Kimchi and Chowder chased after it.

"Hey, come back!" called Chowder.

Chowder finally caught up with his hat and lifted it up.

A very small blue person with horns was clinging to the underside of it. "Whoa, whoa," whoaed Chestnut.

"Chestnut, you found my hat for me!" said Chowder.

"Oh, no, no, *nonononono,*" said Chestnut. "This isn't your hat, Chowder. This is Chestnut's new holiday home."

"But the hat's got my name written inside it in mustard," Chowder protested. "Look!"

Chestnut looked inside the hat and saw a mess of bright yellow scrawl. It could have spelled out Charliekins. Or Chipmunk. Or even Chestnut. "That's just a bunch of gobbledygook," said Chestnut.

Chowder smiled. "Yeah, Mung Daal calls my handwriting 'tragic'," he said proudly. "He compliments me like that all the time."

Chowder went to take his hat back, but Chestnut wasn't about to give it up. "Let go," Chestnut warned. "Chestnut found this holiday home first. Legally, it belongs to Chestnut."

"But ..." said Chowder.

"It's the law," said Chestnut.

"But ..." said Chowder.

"You gonna break the law?" challenged Chestnut.

"No, but ..." repeated Chowder.

"Dirty little law-breaker! Dirty little law-breaker!" Chestnut shouted.

"Stop! That's not me. I'm not that," said Chowder. Then he started to cry. "Can I – **gulp!** – at least say – **sob!** – goodbye?"

Chestnut sighed. "OK," he said. "But no crying. Chestnut doesn't want a flooded basement in his new home."

Chestnut hopped out of his hat-home, and Chowder picked it up.

"So I guess this is it, Hat," said Chowder sadly, stroking it gently. "You've chosen the carefree life of a holiday home and I'm left here alone with my dreams."

Chowder's eyes filled with tears again as he thought about the good times they'd shared. He hugged his hat tightly, and laughed. "Hey, d'you remember when we cooked our first egg together? Good times."

Chestnut was getting impatient. "Hurry it up," he said.

"I'll miss you, Hat," said Chowder. "I'll miss the way you're all pointy on top and I'll miss the way you absorb my sweat when I'm sweaty. And I'll miss getting ear infections cos you're so dirty. And I'll miss – **burp!** – oh, excuse me, that was lunch ... And I'll miss how we would send each other postcards. You know, the ones with pictures of cats wearing little tutus. And I'll miss ..."

By now, Chestnut was fed up. "No, no, *nonononono*," he said. "No more sad talking. Chestnut's heart isn't made out of stone."

"Is it made out of blood?" asked Chowder.

Chestnut ignored him. "Listen, Chestnut's going to make you a sweet deal."

A sweet deal? thought Chowder, as happy thoughts of candies and bars and chews and chocolate filled his head. "I love sweet deals ..." he said.

Chestnut smiled a greedy little smile.

Chapter Three

Chestnut explained the deal that would get Chowder his hat back. "Chestnut will trade you his holiday home for a hydrofoil," he announced.

"A hydrofoil?" repeated Chowder.

"A hydrofoil," Chestnut confirmed.

Chowder had no idea what a hydrofoil was. So, "What's a hydrofoil?" he asked.

Chestnut pointed to the left. "That there's a hydrofoil."

Chowder looked, but he only saw Ancho the dog-man carrying a bright green briefcase.

"It's the rectangle with the handle and buckles," said Chestnut helpfully.

"Ah, so *that's* a hydrofoil," said Chowder, humoring him. He really wanted his hat back.

"Chestnut's gonna look so fly riding in that," said Chestnut, picturing himself as a fly. But a really cool-looking one.

Chowder walked up to Ancho and grabbed his briefcase. Hydrofoil. *Whatever*.

Naturally, this came as quite a surprise to Ancho. "Little plump child," he cried, "what are you doing with my briefcase?"

Wasn't it obvious? "I need to trade this hydrofoil of yours for a holiday home," Chowder explained.

Ancho grabbed the briefcase back. "Away with you," he shooed.

"But, Mister, I need that to get my hat back," said Chowder, starting to cry. "Boo-hoo!"

"Hat?" echoed Ancho. "Say no more of the word. If I lost *my* hat, I, too, would cry like a little, fat boy. My hat would be no ordinary hat! It is a hat of love, of passion ..."

"Wow," said Chowder. He was impressed. This

was some fancy hat talk that Ancho was talking.

"It would be the hat that will finally get me a girlfriend," babbled Ancho. "She will see my hat and say, 'Oh, Ancho, how I love your hat. You must come and snuggle with me.'" He hugged himself happily at the very thought. "Snuggle, snuggle, ooh, snuggle, yes. Ooh, yes! This girlfriend, she will be mine! Listen up, little tubby child. If you get me a girlfriend, I will give you my briefcase so you can have your hat back," he decided.

"Are you sure I can't just have it for free?" asked Chowder.

Ancho ignored that. "Look," he said, pointing to a pig lady who was looking at some fruit on a market stall. "She's right over there. She is the flower that has won my heart."

The pig lady grunted – **grunt-grunt!** – smelled a piece of fruit – **sniff-snuffle!** – and showed it to her dog.

"Her?" asked Chowder, baffled. She didn't look much like girlfriend material to him. She just looked like a pig.

"Yes," said Ancho. "She is truly the boat of my dreams. Go, little fat one, go and get her for me.

Do this and a thousand briefcases shall be yours."

So Chowder went up to the pig lady, who was holding the fruit for her dog to lick.

"Excuse me, Miss?" he said, tugging her dress. "Miss? Uh, *Miss*?"

When she took no notice, he yelled, "Hey, lady!" as loudly as he could.

That got the pig lady's attention. Startled, she pointed at Chowder and grunted angrily. "Get him, Mr Muffintops!" she told her mean-looking dog.

"Grrrrr! Ruff! Gruff! I'll get you, man," growled

Mr Muffintops, leaping at Chowder. "Ruff! Gruff! Grrrrr!"

GROWL! SNAP! NiP! BiTE! GNAW! This was not a fair fight.

"Argh!" cried Chowder between bites. "Lady, all I need is for you to go on a date! Ooo! Oww! Ouch!"

"Oh, you're much too young for me," the pig lady giggled.

"Grrrr!" growled Mr Muffintops, busy chewing Chowder's arm. **RUFF! GRUFF! RiP! TEAR!**

"No, with *that* guy," said Chowder, pointing with his free hand.

"Oh, he's much too short for me," cooed the pig lady, looking at Chestnut.

"No, not *him*," said Chowder, pointing at Ancho again, who was waving and grinning at her. *"Him!"*

"Ooh," laughed the pig lady, waving back at Ancho. "Ooh, well, uh, he *is* cute. OK, but first I need you to do me a little favour ..."

"Anything," said Chowder, who really wanted the arm-mangling to stop.

"You see, Mr Muffintops wore his little self out just now," tittered the pig lady.

Mr Muffintops let go of Chowder's arm to agree. "Grrr! Woof! I need liquid refreshment, man," he panted.

"He needs liquid refreshment," repeated the pig lady. "And Mr Muffintops is very picky. He'll only drink mountain-spring water."

"Grrr! Ruff! Water!" the dog woofed. "I – ruff! – need – gruff! – some – woof! – water!"

"Mountain-spring water?" asked Chowder.

"Woof!" barked Mr Muffintops. "Grrr!"

"Where am I gonna find a mountain?" wondered Chowder.

His question was answered when, suddenly,

a huge two-legged mountain walked by – **clump, clomp, thump, thomp!**

Chowder didn't know where the mountain was heading, but he chased after it anyway. It was the only way to get his hat back!

Chapter Four

Chowder followed the mountain to a high cliff and climbed to the top, where he found a deep, cool pool. "Cold, delicious, mountain-spring water," he gasped, producing a glass.

He was just about to fill the glass when an ogre appeared.

"Halt," rumbled the ogre. "That be my spring, my water. None shall take it."

Chowder ignored him, and went to dip the glass again.

"None shall take it," repeated the ogre.

Chowder went to dip the glass again.

"None shall take it," repeated the ogre.

Chowder went to dip the glass again.

"None shall take it," repeated the ogre.

Chowder went to dip the glass again.

"None shall take it," said the ogre, one more time. He sounded rather tired of the way the conversation was going. "What part of 'none shall take it' do you not understand?"

Chowder went to dip again, and this time the ogre snatched the glass. "Gimme that!" he said angrily. "What is *wrong* with you?"

Chowder told him. "Mister Ogre, I need the water so that the pig lady will date Ancho who'll give me a hydrofoil so that I can give it to Chestnut and get my hat back!"

"Hmm. I'm detecting a pattern here," said the ogre. "All right, then. Bring me a fancy tea set and you shall have your water."

"OK," said Chowder, trying to get straight what he needed as he walked away. "Tea set, tea set, tea set, tea set, tea set, tea set …"

When Chowder found a building shaped like a giant teapot with a teapot-shaped sign that said

THE TEAPOT, he guessed this might be a good place to swap for a tea set. But it wasn't quite that simple. In Chowder's world, it never was.

"If you want a tea set, you must trade me for a red yo-yo," sang the tea shop lady, so Chowder set off again. And again. And *again*. At each of Chowder's stops all over Marzipan City, a new swapper joined in a swapperific song.

"For my yo-yo, I want snow boots ..." sang the yo-yo man.

"Which I'll trade for some duct tape ..." sang the boot man at his shop.

"Which I'll trade for tweezers ..." sang the duct tape man.

"Then I'll trade you for one oven glove ..." sang the tweezer man.

"For some lip balm ..." sang the glove man.

"New cough drops ..." sang the lip balm man.

"A baseball made with some love ..." sang the cough drop man.

"I want a flashy writing pen ..." sang the loving baseball man.

"And trousers with some attitude ..." sang the pen man.

"Does asking for a magic pickle mean that I am being shrewd?" sang the trouser man.

"I'll trade a magic pickle cos my head is sunburned and I really need a hat ..." sang the pickle man.

A hat? A HAT? He knew just where to find one! Chowder ran back to find Chestnut. "Hey, Chestnut," he said, "to get your hydrofoil, I'm gonna need your hat."

"Holiday home," Chestnut corrected.

"Right," said Chowder.

"OK, but Chestnut's got his eye on you," warned Chestnut.

"One, two, three," counted Chowder. The trading was about to begin.

One by one, all the different items people wanted were swapped. All the swappers sang:

> This for that and that for this
> And these for those and those for these
> And that and that and these for that
> And this and this and these for those
> A yo-yo for a tea set
> And spring water for a date with Ancho
> Last not least the hydrofoil
> For Chestnut who's about to boil.

As they sang, a giant eyedropper came down from the sky and dripped water into Mr Muffintops' bowl. "Rrrrrr," he growled, lapping happily.

Finally, most of the swaps were done. With a happy grunt, the pig lady leapt into Ancho's arms and he carried the final swap over to Chestnut – the green briefcase, as agreed. Everyone went off on their merry way, except for ...

"Wait," said Chowder. Something wasn't quite right, but he didn't know what. "Did the song say 'last not least'?"

What about Chowder's swap?

Where was his hat?

Chapter Five

Chowder saw that the pickle man had the hat.
The purple hat. With bumps and lumps. The
smelly hat. *His* hat. "Right," he said. "Uh, Pickle
Man, I need that hat back."

"OK," said the pickle man. "But I'll need my
magic pickle back."

Off they went again. It was time for more
swaps and trades, and more singing.

**This for that and that for this
And these for those and those for these.**

At the end of all that swapping, Chowder was gasping for breath. "Done!" he said.

Then he saw Chestnut standing by the hat. "Mine," Chestnut told him.

"Rats!" said Chowder.

That swap hadn't worked out quite right, so he started all over again, and this time the traders sang even louder.

**And that and that and these for that
And this and this and these for those.**

This time, the pig lady ended up wearing
Chowder's hat. It didn't look good.

"Rats!" said Chowder. They tried again.

**This for that and that for this
And these for those and those for these.**

Now the smelly man was wearing the hat.

"Rats!" said Chowder as he started the
swapping again.

Each time the residents of Marzipan City
sang the song, they swapped items and changed
places. But somehow or other Chowder never got
the one thing he wanted …

And that for that.

"Rats!"

And these for that.

"Rats!"

And this for this.

"Rats!"

And these for those.

"Rats!"

Many hours and many swaps (and many sore throats) later, Chowder's boss, Mung Daal, was in the kitchen of his catering company when Chowder and Kimchi arrived.

Chowder was grinning from ear to ear, and he had his hat back on his head at last.

"Well, don't you look happy," said Mung.

Faarpy-faarp-faarp-faarp-faarp! went Kimchi, which was his way of saying, 'Yes, he does look rather happy, doesn't he?'

"I got my hat back," said Chowder. "It's like a little part of me died inside, and now it's come back to life."

Just then, Shnitzel the rock monster walked by. "Radda-radda-radda-radda," he said.

Chowder understood. "What do you mean, you're '*still* dead inside'?" he asked.

Mung ignored them both and declared, "I think this calls for a celebration dance!" He, Chowder, Shnitzel and Kimchi started to jig and float around the kitchen.

As they danced, Chestnut poked his head out from under Chowder's hat.

"Earthquake! It's an earthquake!" he screamed.

"We're just dancing," explained Chowder.

"Well, knock it off," snarled Chestnut, popping back under the hat. "Chestnut is trying to get some shut-eye. Chestnut'll take his mobile home somewhere else if you can't be quiet."

"Yes, sir, Mr Chestnut, sir!" Chowder said.

Mung raised a bushy eyebrow.

"Oh, yeah, I forgot to tell you, Mung," confided Chowder. "I can keep my hat as long as we never make any noise. Not a sound. Not a whisper. Never. Never again. Never ever."

But it was all worth it. "I'm glad to have you back, Hat," Chowder murmured lovingly.

"Quiet!" yelled Chestnut from underneath.

"Sorry," smiled Chowder. "*Sshhhhh ...*"

And Chowder, Chestnut and their mobile-home hat lived happily (and silently) ever after.

THE END

Chowder's hat passes by.

Chestnut's new holiday home.

Chowder takes Ancho's briefcase.

Mr Muffintops needs a drink.

STINKY LOVE GALLERY

A smelly start to the day for Chowder.

Kimchi likes chocolate Thrice Cream.

Shnitzel sniffs a stink!

The Upper Highland
Marfhillforgerlurger
dance.

Kimchi floats off with
the clabbage cobbler.

Shnitzel to the rescue!

A stinky surprise!

People queue (and dance) for clabbage cobblers.

Stinky Love

Chapter One

One morning in Marzipan City, Chowder was fast asleep in his bedroom at the top of Mung Daal's Catering Company tower, snoring gently. Surprise, surprise – Chowder was dreaming about food. "Why yes, I would love third helpings, thank you," he mumbled happily.

Kimchi, Chowder's pet stink cloud, woke up and floated out of his cage. **Faarp!** He landed on Chowder's face and made one of his super-stinky, pong-whiffy smells. Chowder breathed in and was suddenly awake. Very wide awake, indeed.

"Good morning, Kimchi," said Chowder. Which was very polite of him, considering the smell.

Faarp! greeted Kimchi. **Faaaarp!**

Even another horrible smell couldn't spoil Chowder's good mood. "Who wants breakfast?"

he sang. "Who wants some breakfast?" There was only one answer to that, and Chowder had it: "I do!"

He took out a bag of food. "Some for me," he said, chomp-chomping happily. "And some for you, Kimchi."

But when Chowder shook some of the food into where he thought Kimchi's mouth was, it passed right through him. Well, he *is* a stink cloud, after all ...

Down in the kitchen, Mung Daal's rock-monster assistant, Shnitzel, was making dough.

"C'mon, Shnitzel," Mung coached. "You've got to really *knead* the dough. I want to be able to taste the elbow."

Just then, Kimchi sneakily floated in and – **fweep!** – made a stink so stinky that Mung's face turned black. Phew, what a pong!

Kimchi floated towards his next victim.

"Nuh, radda-radda-radda-da," objected Shnitzel, holding his nose as Kimchi whiffed around him.

Fweep! went Kimchi.

Chowder arrived just in time to see what his stinky pet was doing. "The faarps and fweeps are just Kimchi's way of saying he likes you," he explained to Mung and Shnitzel. "Wanna hear his way of saying he has to go potty?"

That would be a *no*, Mung decided. He needed to get the smelly cloud out of his sniffing range. "Er, Chowder," he said to his apprentice, "why don't you take Kimchi to the Farmers' Market and pick up some clabbages for me?"

Faarp! went Kimchi.

"Got it," agreed Chowder. "C'mon, Kimchi."

Faarpy-faarp-faarp! went Kimchi as they left.

It was safe to breathe again. "Wow," said

Mung. "The smells some people put up with."

"Tell me about it …" said his mushroom-fairy wife, Truffles, as she flew by.

"Clabbages, clabbages, gotta get some clabbages," Chowder sang as he strolled through the streets with Kimchi floating along beside him.

When Chowder and Kimchi saw a yak sitting on a bench eating a Thrice-Cream cone, they both stopped and stared.

"Can I help you?" asked the yak in mid-lick.

"That looks good," drooled Chowder, his eyes locked on the melting goodness.

"Yeah, it is," said the yak, taking another lick. "You gonna stare at me all day?"

"Is that chocolate?" asked Chowder.

"Yeah," said the yak.

"I like chocolate," mentioned Chowder hopefully.

"Good for you," said the yak. "Look, kid, don't make me call the po–"

Before the yak could finish, Kimchi floated onto the Thrice Cream, and – **faarp-faarpy-faarp-faarp!** – made super-rude noises. And smells.

"Kimchi likes chocolate, too," explained Chowder.

Yuck! What a pong! The yak sniffed, disgusted. "Oh, crud," he snapped, walking away. "Well, now you've ruined my Thrice Cream with your stink. Stupid stink cloud. This used to be a nice part of town."

Stupid stink cloud? **Fluurp!** went Kimchi sadly.

Chowder frowned. Hey, stink clouds had feelings, too!

Chapter Two

In the Farmer's Market, Chowder's friend, Gazpacho, was talking to a pig customer at his fruit and vegetable stall.

"You know how you can tell these are ripe?" he said, pointing to a box of fruit. "See the green ones?"

The pig looked. They were all green.

"The green ones are fresh," Gazpacho told him.

"These?" said the pig, holding up a green fruit.

"No," Gazpacho said. "That one's obviously *yellow*-green."

The pig tried to find a ripe one. He picked one up.

"No," said Gazpacho.

The pig picked another.

"No."

The pig picked another.

"No."

The pig picked another.

"Ye– no."

The pig picked another.

"No."

The pig picked another.

"No."

The pig picked another.

"Yes! Now pick that one up and smell it. No, the other end ..."

The customer sniffed at the same instant that Kimchi floated in front of his nose, and –
fluurp! – let go another bad smell.

The pig coughed, spluttered and choked, then fell to the ground in stinky-smell shock.

"Oh dear," mourned Gazpacho as Chowder walked up to the stall, stepping over the stunned customer.

"Hello, Chowder," said Gazpacho, wearily.

"Hi, Gazpacho," Chowder replied. "I need to pick up some clabbages for Mung."

Gazpacho smiled. "Chowder, you know you're my little dude, right?" he said in an I-like-you-very-much-BUT kind of voice.

"Riiiightt ..." said Chowder uneasily.

"But I made the sign for a reason," Gazpacho said, pointing to a huge poster of Kimchi with a big red mark drawn across him. The meaning was obvious. Kimchi Banned. No Kimchi. Kimchi Not Allowed. Never. Ever. Never-ever.

"Oh, sorry," said Chowder. "C'mon, Kimchi."

Fluuuurp! went Kimchi pitifully, and floated after his owner.

After many tries, Chowder finally found a clabbage seller who wasn't so anti-stink. On the way back to work, he tried to make his friend feel better. "Don't worry, Kimchi," said Chowder soothingly. "Even though everyone says you stink, I still like you."

Faarpy-faarp! went Kimchi gratefully.

Back at Mung Daal's, "I've got the clabbages," Chowder announced.

"Oh, great," said Mung.

Chowder looked, then looked again, blinked, and stared. Mung and Shnitzel were wearing weird suits in a shade of purple best described as WARNING: SUNGLASSES NEEDED. Shoulder straps held up huge, baggy clown pants. The look was topped off with bright red, bottom-shaped hats on their heads.

"W-what're you wearing?" stammered Chowder.

"Chowder, do you know what 'tradition' means?" asked Mung.

"Is it one of those things where I have to leave the room while you talk about it?"

"No," said Mung. "Tradition is the tucked-in napkin in the shirt of society."

That didn't tell Chowder an awful lot. "So why are you wearing those clothes?" he persisted.

"We got an order for a traditional Upper Highland Marfhillforgerlurger dish called a clabbage cobbler," Mung explained.

"Oooooh …" said Chowder. He was trying to sound as though he understood, but really, he had no idea what his boss was talking about.

"And tradition dictates that we must wear these Upper Highland Marfhillforgerlurger costumes when making the clabbage cobbler," added Mung.

Shnitzel was looking a little worried. "Radda-radda-radda?" he asked.

"No, the outfit doesn't make your bum look big …" fibbed Mung, rolling his eyes. Rock monsters could be so *sensitive*.

Chapter Three

Later, Mung, Shnitzel and Chowder got busy
making the clabbage cobbler.

As it bubbled – **shlurp-shlop!** – a thick, green,
smelly cloud floated up from the cooking pot.
And this time, it wasn't Kimchi.

"First, we stew up the clabbages to make them
nice and stinky," said Mung.

Next, the clabbages were squeezed, softened
and plopped into a big bowl. **Splat! Sploosh!**

"Now we load 'em into the traditional clabbage smasher," Mung explained, as another bowl dropped down and smashed the clabbages to a pulp. **Slop! Glop!** As they got sloppier and gloppier, more stinky clouds of gas rose up into the air.

"Radda ..." Shnitzel groaned, meaning 'that smell is just awful'. But as he could only say one thing, he said that instead. "Radda!"

Mung Daal sniffed. "You think it smells bad now?" he said. "Wait until we add the traditional glumburger cheese."

Now just how bad could cheese smell? thought Chowder. Sniff, sniff! "Grughhh! he groaned as his face crumpled, shrank and melted, and he got his answer: Very. Very. Bad.

"Sometimes it's hard to tell the difference between good cheese and bad feet," remarked Mung as he and Shnitzel held each end of a long saw and began slicing up a giant onion.

The fumes from the onion were so strong that they made Mung and Shnitzel cry like – well, like Mung and Shnitzel.

"Boo-hoo-hoooo," sobbed Mung.

"Radda-radda-raaaadda," blubbed Shnitzel.

Between wails, Mung ordered Chowder to get a bucket to collect the salty tears.

Mung poured them into the cobbler. "And finally, some traditional tears," he declared, and the kitchen filled with more smelly green gas. "It peels the skin off your eyeballs, doesn't it?"

"Radda-radda-radda!" The gas was so strong that Shnitzel could hardly breathe. Coughing and spluttering, he opened the window to let some fresh air in and some smelly gas out.

The green stench fumes rose up into the air and straight into Chowder's bedroom window.

Kimchi was inside, napping in his cage, though it would take more than bars of steel to contain a stink cloud as potent as him. As the fumes drifted past, he took one sniff and – **faarp-faarp!** – made a rude noise. **Fweep!** What a wonderful whiff! **Fluurp!** How powerfully pongy! He and the smellicious smell were made for each other!

Back in the kitchen, Mung held up the dish of the finished clabbage cobbler. "Ah," he sighed, taking a nice, deep sniff. "Now, while this ferments, we must perform the traditional Upper Highland Marfhillforgerlurger dance."

Ear-achingly awful music blared as Mung, Shnitzel and Chowder hop-danced around on one leg, fingers in noses, their puffy red hats bobbing up and down.

As they danced, Kimchi floated in. He had followed the trail of the gorgeously ghastly smell down to the clabbage cobbler dish.

Kimchi circled the dish. He could not resist it. Sniff-sniffy-sniff-sniff! You've heard of love at first sight? Well, this was love at first sniff.

"Hey, Kimchi's doing the dance, too," smiled Chowder.

Faarp! went Kimchi, floating around the dish and gazing at it lovingly. **Faaarp! Faaaaarp!**

Then he landed on the dish – and floated off with it!

"Kimchi, no!" cried Chowder.

"What's he doing?" asked Mung in a panic as his clabbage cobbler exited the kitchen, stolen by a love-struck stink cloud.

Faaarp! went Kimchi. **Faaaaarp!**

"Kimchi!" called Chowder, chasing after his runaway pet.

"My cobbler!" cried Mung, hot on his heels.

"Radda-radda," added Shnitzel, bringing up the rear.

Faarp! went Kimchi as he floated high up with his beloved cobbler. **Faarp! Fweep! Fluurp!**

"Oh dear, this isn't part of the tradition," said Mung. "Shnitzel, you've got to get him down."

Question one: How does a rock monster get a stink cloud to give back a kidnapped dish of clabbage cobbler?

Answer: By throwing rocks at it. *Large* rocks.

Question two: How does a stink cloud avoid being hit by the rocks?

Answer: By dodging them.

Faarpy-faarp! went Kimchi. Missed!

"Careful, Shnitzel," warned Mung as Kimchi escaped to the rooftop of the Catering Company. "You'll hurt the dish."

Chowder had to do something …

"Kimchi!" he gasped, climbing up the steps that snaked around the tower.

"Wait, Chowder!" said Mung.

But Chowder just carried on climbing.

"Kimchi? You've got to come back down," he told his pet when he got to the top.

Faarp! Faarp! Faarp! Kimchi just made happy

I-love-you-my-smelly-little-angel type noises, ignoring everything else.

"Huh?" said Chowder. He was beginning to see why Kimchi was acting so weirdly. Weirdly for a stink cloud, that is.

Faarp! Faarp! Kimchi made more I-love-you-my-smelly-little-angel noises.

"Chowder! Is the clabbage cobbler OK?" Mung called from below.

"Yes," answered Chowder. Then he made a decision. A big one. And Mung was not going to be very happy about it ...

Chapter Four

"I'm leaving the clabbage cobbler with Kimchi!" Chowder yelled down from the tower.

Mung exploded in fury. "What?" he cried. *Was the kid mad?*

"I think they're in love," Chowder explained.

Mung tried to sound patient. "Chowder, I understand being in love with a cobbler more than anyone," he said. "But we've got a customer who expects the dish to come love-*free*."

"But the dish makes Kimchi happy," said Chowder. And Kimchi's happiness was worth getting in trouble for. "Don't worry. I'll make sure nothing happens to it."

Mung turned to Shnitzel. "You got any ideas?" Silly question.

"No! No more rocks!" cried Mung, as Shnitzel produced an enormous boulder. "Everything is *rocks* with you. Just go up and get it."

Shnitzel put down the rock and climbed to the top of the next-door tower. A thick chain joined it to Mung's tower, but Shnitzel wasn't keen on the idea of walking across it. After all, rock monsters weren't exactly built for tightrope-walking ...

But it had to be done. "Radda?" Shnitzel gulped, breaking into a sweat as he stood on the chain and took his first wibbly-wobbly step.

"Shnitzel, just don't think about falling," Mung told him helpfully. "Or slipping. Or plummeting. Or gravity. Or losing your balance. And especially don't think about ..."

"*Radda!*" cried Shnitzel, flapping his arms to try to keep his balance. Then he wobbled, lost his footing and slipped, but managed to grab onto the chain just in time.

Mung gasped as he watched Shnitzel start to haul himself along the chain toward the tower, panting hard as he moved from link to link.

"Raddaaa ..." he moaned in fear.

Unfortunately for Shnitzel, Mung had more advice. "OK, now don't think about losing your grip, or how sweaty your hands are ..." he called.

As Shnitzel got close to Mung's tower, Chowder suddenly appeared above him. "Hey, Shnitzel!" he yelled.

Startled, Shnitzel lost his grip, screamed –
"Raaa-*daaa*!" – and hurtled towards the ground.

"Darn," said Chowder. "I thought he was
coming to keep us company, Kimchi."

Mung could only look on as Shnitzel hit a roof
– **thump!** – then the ground – **bump!** – and rolled
like a big, grey marble through the streets of
Marzipan City, yelping as he banged into walls
and doors.

CLUMP! BUMP! THUMP! Truffles came flying out
when she heard the racket.

"What's with all the yelling?" she enquired.

"Well, you see –" said Mung.

"I don't wanna hear it," snapped Truffles. "Just make the na-na-na-na-na-na-na stop!"

"Don't worry, honey," cooed Mung. "Your he-man will handle it."

"I don't have time to wait for him," said Truffles. "*You* do it."

Which is why Mung found himself trying to climb a drainpipe. He got just one step off the ground before he stopped, grunting and gasping, as sweat rolled down his face.

Just then, Mung's clabbage cobbler customer arrived. "'Allo. My order of clabbage cobbler ees ready, yes?" he asked in the weird Upper Highland Marfhillforgerlurger accent. "I hop on leg all way here, as is tradition."

"Ah, yes," wheezed Mung as he clung to the wall. "Tradition. Even though it goes against tradition, the dish won't be ready until … tomorrow morning."

The customer stopped hopping. "You ees kidding," he said. "I been hopping for six hours."

"I'm sorry. We'll try to have it for you tomorrow," said Mung.

"OK," said the customer.

Truffles was irate at having to turn away a valuable customer. No cobbler meant no money! "When you get down," she shouted up at Chowder, "you're getting such a bop on the noggin!"

"If you get hungry, don't eat the cobbler!" added Mung. "Eat bricks or something!"

Truffles glared at her husband so fiercely, his blue skin instantly tanned to a lovely purple. Mung trembled with fright. How was he going to rescue the cobbler by tomorrow?

Chapter Five

That night, as darkness fell over Marzipan City, Chowder was still on top of the tower with Kimchi and the clabbage cobbler.

"Wow," said Chowder, looking out over the twinkling lights. "The city is so pretty from up here. Kimchi, come and look at ..."

Kimchi wasn't listening. He was purring softly – **fluuuuur!** – never taking his lovesick eyes from the cobbler he adored.

"Don't worry, Kimchi," Chower reassured him. "Your love is safe as long as I'm up here."

Fweep! Fluurp! went Kimchi insistently.

Chowder took the hint. "OK, I'm gonna give you two some privacy," he said.

Faarp-faarp! Fweep! Fluurp! went Kimchi, blowing super-smelly, heart-shaped gassy kisses at the dish.

Chowder yawned. "Goodnight, Kimchi," he whispered, and soon the only sound that could be heard were his snores. **Zzzzzzz ...**

Faarp! Fweep! Fluurp! And Kimchi's farps ...

In the morning, Chowder woke up and looked around. *Yikes!* He was surrounded by eggs – thousands of them.

Eggs are for eating, right? thought Chowder. *Right.* "Whoa!" he smiled, cramming five into his mouth and chomping happily. "Somebody brought me breakfast."

Then, "Huh?" he said, as the shell of one of the uneaten eggs slowly **c-r-a-c-k-e-d** open and out came ...

"A mini clabbage cobbler!" he gasped.

One by one, the eggs cracked open and little baby cobblers hatched out – thousands of them!

"Kimchi! Kimchi!" gabbled Chowder. "Look! It's a miracle."

Kimchi woke up and looked around, alarmed and amazed at becoming a dad to thousands of clabbage cobblers. He farped loudly in shock – **fluurp!** – then fell over in a smelly faint.

"I guess miracles make Kimchi sleepy," said Chowder. He grabbed one of the cobblers and rushed down to the kitchen.

"Mung, look, look!" he cried. "The big stinky clabbage cobbler made lots of little stinky clabbage cobblers."

Mung bit into one, pan and all, chewed, and made an I-like-that-a-lot-it's-very-yummy noise. "Incredible," he said. "Are there any more of these?"

"Oh, yeah!" Chowder said.

News of the many-mini clabbage cobblers soon spread, and the citizens of Marzipan City all formed a long queue to get their paws on the stinky treats. They were all dressed in the weird Upper Highland Marfhillforgerlurger costumes and hopped on one foot as they waited their turn.

Truffles set up a stall outside to serve them. "Mini clabbage cobblers!" she yelled. "Come get 'em while they're little and stinky."

The baby cobblers might have been small in size, but they sure smelled mightily.

"Radda," said Shnitzel as the gas reached him. Phew-eee! What a pong!

When Mung spotted his original customer, he handed him the big mummy cobbler, which Shnitzel had managed to snatch from Kimchi. "Thank you for your patience," Mung smiled.

"No, zank *you*," replied the customer. "In Upper Highland Marfhillforgerlurger, we haf a saying about the patience." He paused.

Mung waited.

And waited.

This better be worth waiting for, thought Mung.

He waited some more.

"It ees *good* to be patient," the Upper Highland Marfhillforgerlurger man finally concluded, then hopped away with his clabbage cobbler.

Er. Right.

Kimchi floated over his mini cobblers and made extra-super-smelly-daddy noises – **faarp! fweep! fluuurp!** – as happy customer number 2,493 hopped home with his stinky treat. The love of Kimchi's life was cruelly taken from him, but he was proud of his popular babies.

And Chowder was proud of his pet. Kimchi had shown that stink clouds should be appreciated, and not just for their silent-but-deadly room-clearing abilities.

"Well, Kimchi, as a ladies' man myself, I can tell you this," said Mung as he approached. "'Tis better to have loved and lost, than never to have loved at all."

"What does that mean?" asked Chowder.

Mung shrugged. "Beats me."

"I *will* if you don't cook up more things to sell," said Truffles in a panic. The cobblers were going fast, and the queue was longer than ever. She needed a backup plan – and quick! She flew up to Kimchi. "There you are, darling," she cooed. "If you're interested, I know a nice casserole that's just your type ..."

Fluuuuurp! went Kimchi. No way – love STINKS!

THE END